THE ELIXIR FIXERS

SASHA AND PUCK
AND THE CORDIAL CORDIAL

BOOK 2

DANIEL NAYERI

ILLUSTRATED BY ANNELIESE MAK

Albert Whitman & Company
Chicago, Illinois

Library of Congress Cataloging-in-Publication
data is on file with the publisher.

Text copyright © 2019 by Daniel Nayeri
Illustrations copyright © 2019 by Anneliese Mak
First published in the United States of America
in 2019 by Albert Whitman & Company
ISBN 978-0-8075-7243-6

Printed in the United States of America
10 9 8 7 6 5 4 3 2 1 LB 24 23 22 21 20 19

Design by Ellen Kokontis

For more information about Albert Whitman & Company,
visit our website at www.albertwhitman.com.

100 years of Albert Whitman & Company
Celebrate with us in 2019!

To Love

MAP OF THE VILLAGE

SPARKSTONE MOUNTAINS

SUNDERDOWN FALLS

THE OLD TREE

A MYSTERIOUS PLACE

CATHEDRAL

GENTRY MANSION

CAKER

SWELTERING RIVER

MAYOR'S HOUSE

CHOCOLATE SHOP

GRANNY YENTA'S HOUSE

JEWELER

THISTLEWOOD SWAMP

SHIVERING RIVER

CENTRAL MARKET

THE JUICY GIZZARD

GROCER

TINKER CART

MILLER

VILLAGE SQUARE

BAKER

COBBLER

VILLAGE GREEN

INN

DOCKS

BLACKSMITH

STABLES

STONE LAKE

WHISPERSHAW CASTLE

THE STORY SO FAR...

Sasha Bebbin lives in a village tucked away in a far-off corner of a world, between the mountains and the sea. She lives with her papa in an alchemy shop named the Juicy Gizzard. Her mother was the alchemist, but she has gone off to help fight against the Make Mad Order.

Now, Papa makes and sells the potions. But he's not a very good alchemist.

And Sasha, who doesn't even believe in magic, is worried that customers will start to complain. Then, Papa will be taken to the constable, who will give them a fine that they cannot afford to pay. And then, the wealthy gruel baron, Vadim Gentry, will buy up the Juicy Gizzard, and Sasha and Papa will be homeless.

And so Sasha has her mission. Along with her sidekick, Puck—a mysterious, wild boy from the woods—Sasha must use her detective skills to investigate the *real* reason every customer wants a potion, whether it's luck or love or just a cure for the hiccups. She has to do this without being discovered. And the hardest part? She has to find a way to make the potion come true, to give the customer the magic they were looking for, before anyone finds out!

CHAPTER 1

Outside, the autumn leaves were red, and the harvest birds were fed.

Inside, Papa was in bed, while Sasha read, and Puck was nearly dead.

Dead with boredom.

Chewing his own arms just for something to do.

"Stop that," said Sasha.

The sound of his smacking was wet and made her anxious.

"Oh, oddity, what is wrong with you?" said Sasha, putting down her book. It was about the wild horses of the hill country, who sang to each other as they galloped across the hills.

Puck continued to chomp on his own arm as if it were a kebab.

The worst part, to Sasha, was that he was such a dirty little creature that biting any part of him would only taste like dirt.

"I will gag if you keep doing that," she said.

He kept doing it.

Sasha sat behind the giant oaken counter of the Juicy Gizzard, *makers of medicines, teas, and alchemies*. That was more true when her mama was around. Papa made the medicines and teas. Mama made the alchemies. And they

would joke that the best tea was any water Sasha dipped her toes in. This was back when she was very little, obviously. Because then, they would pretend to chomp on her toes. It would be gross now if they did that. She was old enough to carry water from the well and gather flowers from the Willow Wood (but not *too* far into the Willow Wood). She could even dry the tea leaves—rose hips, chamomile, and hibiscus—by herself.

Puck lay on the floor with his arm in his mouth. He was so much like an animal that Sasha wondered if he'd been raised by wolves. And not particularly smart wolves either.

They had spent the morning tending the shop and listening to the crows cawing at each other about the best fields to pillage. There were no customers. They had fewer and fewer these days. It made Sasha worry. But Papa didn't seem to mind. "More time for reading," he'd say.

But already, he was counting coins and cutting thinner slices of cheese for his flatbread. She knew he had stopped taking sugar with his tea in the mornings. And she knew he stayed up late into the nights, outside with the cauldron, boiling turpentine, oil scum, fish scales, bark from rotted trees, and fox fat to make a liniment for making horses go to sleep. It was a foul-smelling job that turned his fingers yellow. But it was good medicine that he could sell to the caravans traveling down the mountains. Their horses and donkeys would be scared or footsore, and the liniment helped them through the long journeys.

And so Papa slept later in the mornings. And Sasha minded the store and felt a bit more at ease, since he wasn't selling magic potions. And Puck...well, that left him with very little to do but fight with Otto, their pig, chase chickens, or bite his own toenails.

"I mean it. I'm gagging now," said Sasha. "Stop it. I can hear the clipping of the nails. And—wait. Are you swallowing them?"

Sasha truly gagged this time. She grabbed a salt rock on the counter and threw it at him. It smacked him on the forehead. Puck yowled like a cat with its tail underfoot.

"Shh," said Sasha.

Puck grabbed up the rock, ready to throw it back.

"Don't," said Sasha, drawing herself up. "You'll wake Papa."

Puck made a bitter grunt.

"If you could read," she said, "you wouldn't be so bored all the time."

"Guh," said Puck with a shrug.

"You should take a lesson from me, Puck. I was reading about horses and entertained myself all morning."

Puck rolled his eyes but scrambled up to the counter and pawed at the book.

"Okay, I'll tell you. There are wild horses in a faraway hill country, where they say some of them are so fast that they burn the grass when they gallop. Those are the Cinderhooves. And some are so graceful that they say flowers grow wherever they roam. Those are the Bloomhooves."

Puck made a whistling sound, though he was mostly toothless.

"I know," said Sasha. "Amazing."

Puck said, "Guh."

"Well, not exactly," said Sasha. "It isn't magic."

"Guh!" insisted Puck.

"No, silly. There's no such thing. It's obvious

the Cinderhooves are flat-footed, and the friction between their hoof and the grass makes it like a rug burn. And the Bloomhooves must get seeds caught in between their hooves that spread wherever they go."

Puck shook his head vigorously. He did not accept her explanation.

"Trust me, Puck," said Sasha, "if you could read, you'd know." She wiped the mud from the counter where his arms had been. "Besides," she said, "if there are such magical horses, why haven't we seen any?"

At that very moment, they heard the sound of four horses clopping into the yard in front of the shop.

Sasha held her breath.

Puck smiled a wily smile and made a satisfied noise.

"Oh hush," said Sasha. "That's just a coincidence."

When the hooves came to a stop right outside the shop door, she said, "I mean, it has to be, right?"

CHAPTER 2

The horses were neither Cinderhooves nor Bloomhooves. They were just horses with regular hooves, pulling a fancy carriage.

Sasha and Puck had run to the window to make sure.

"Told you," said Sasha. "What are the odds that magic horses would arrive today of all days?"

"Meh," said Puck. He was already finished with that topic and had become interested in the carriage, which seemed to have a compartment in the back stocked with bags of cheese sticks, cinnamon bread, and boxes of Mrs. Kozlow's famous bonbons.

On the door of the carriage was a lacy, gold seal. Sasha knew it very well.

"Don't get any ideas about them sharing those groceries," she said. "That's the Gentry carriage."

Puck huffed out his disappointment. They watched as the door of the carriage opened. Out stepped Basil Gentry, a tall and thin young man with kind and contented eyes. He never seemed to be in a hurry and always seemed to be smiling.

He was the Gentry that Sasha liked most. But he was still a Gentry. "Quick," she said. "Act busy."

She could never let a Gentry see that business was slow, not with Vadim looking to buy the shop. Sasha ran behind the counter and made a show of weighing each salt rock on a brass scale and handing it to Puck for packing.

The door opened to the chime of Mama's glass bell, and Basil entered.

Sasha looked up from her task. "Be right with you," she said. "We're just finishing up."

"Uh, okay," said Basil. "Are you—"

"Very busy," said Sasha. "One moment." She handed Puck the last salt rock. Then she looked over and saw him take it, lick it, and stick it to his forehead—beside all the others. His whole face was pocked with salt rocks. His eyes were wide with innocence. He looked back and forth from Sasha to Basil, as if the trick was working.

"What in the name of fiffle faffle are you doing?" said Sasha. "Gimme those."

Puck still didn't seem to understand. He took

a salt rock from his cheek and tried to stick it to Sasha's face instead.

"No. Okay, go sit in the corner."

Puck's dirty, salt-rock-covered forehead made an angry frown. He stomped over to the corner of the shop, slapped the rocks from his face, and kicked them all around before slumping to the ground.

Sasha tried to regain her composure. "We were just checking those rocks for...um..."

She couldn't think of anything. "Poison," she said finally.

"You had your gremlin licking rocks to see if they were poisonous?" said Basil.

"Yes. He's not mine, and he's not a gremlin. I think he's just a dirty woodland child. But yes."

"And what if one *was* poison?" said Basil.

"Oh. Right. Well, we'd give him the magic antidote. We're an alchemy shop, after all. These bottles have dozens of cures." She waved her

arms at the shelves of bottles in all shapes and colors.

"That's why I've come, actually," said Basil. "I'd like to buy a potion...a magic potion."

Crumbsy bumsy, thought Sasha.

"Have you thought about tea instead?" said Sasha. "There are very few things that a cup of tea can't fix."

"I'm afraid this is one of them."

"We don't make curses, you know."

"It's not a curse."

"And you should know your face is already very handsome."

Basil turned red. His sister, Sisal, had given him the name Bashful Basil for a reason.

"I only mean that there's no need for magic arts. Your nose, the eyes, hair, all of it—it's working."

"That's good to hear," said Basil.

"So you'll have some tea, then? Maybe some horse liniment? It's boiling up fresh in the back."

"No."

"No?"

"No, thank you."

"What do you mean, no?"

"I mean I've come for a magic potion. Not a curse. Not for my face."

"Oh," said Sasha. She had run out of strategies.

"I'd like some magic, please, that makes a person more polite. Nothing too much. No sucking up. Just courtesy. I'd like it to make someone courteous."

"Wow. Hmm. Okay. That's very complicated."

"Neh neh neh!" shouted Puck from the corner, arms crossed, still pouting.

"No. I do not need that potion myself," said Sasha. "And I don't think we have any anyway." She pretended to look around the overstuffed shelves, pushing aside the ones in front to read the labels of the ones behind.

"Of course we have it," said Papa. His voice entered the room before he did. He was still in his pajamas and nightcap.

"Of all the odds and oddity!" said Sasha under her breath.

"Young master Gentry is looking for a cordial cordial," said Papa. "I made a batch just last week with lily ash and spit from an insulted llama."

"Are those good ingredients for a cordial cordial?" asked Basil.

"The very best," said Papa, reaching up to a corner shelf to grab the bottle. "I added sassafras, which actually *reduces* sass, and blackberries."

"Do the blackberries do something special?"

"Yes, they make it taste like blackberries. That'll be seven pieces."

Basil reached into his coin pouch and handed Papa seven coins.

"Thank you," said Basil. "This is a great help. You have no idea how much this will help." Basil tucked the bottle into his coat pocket and turned to leave.

Sasha wondered why Basil, of all people, needed a cordial cordial. He was already so polite. He had even said "please" and "thank you" as he bought it.

It was shaping up to be a mystery. And she would have to solve it fast. It was up to her to make the potion come true. As Basil said goodbye, Sasha grabbed her satchel and ran out with him. "Gotta go, Papa. Love you!"

Puck grunted and followed right on her heels.

"Wait," said Papa. "Where are you going? Did you eat breakfast? And what happened to my salt rocks?"

CHAPTER 3

When Basil opened the door of the carriage, he stepped back and knocked into Sasha. She was standing right behind him.

"Hi, Basil."

Basil looked confused. "I'm sorry. I thought we did this part already."

"I thought maybe I could join you."

"Do you need a lift? Where are you going?"

"I'm going your way?"

"I'm going home."

"Right, that direction, I mean."

"Toward the village?"

"Yeah."

"Okay."

So they both jumped into the carriage. As soon as they closed the door, the dirty head of Puck appeared in the window. Then it dropped out of sight. Then it appeared again. Then out again. Then in again.

Sasha and Basil sat across from each other in the carriage, trying not to notice Puck jumping up and down outside, shouting, "Guh! Guh!"

Finally, Sasha said, "Excuse me one second."

She opened the window and whispered as forcefully as she could, "You can't come in."

"Guh!"

"Because the seats are made of silk, and you're made of mud and boogers."

Puck stuck his tongue out and blew a furious raspberry.

Sasha closed the window and plopped back into her seat.

Basil knocked on the roof to let the driver know they were ready. The team of horses trotted out. Behind them, Puck scrambled on all fours and jumped onto the back of the carriage with the groceries.

"I've never been in a carriage before," said Sasha.

"I would have walked, but we had to get a lot of stuff."

Basil seemed almost embarrassed by the fancy carriage.

"Are you throwing a party?" asked Sasha. Maybe that was why he needed the cordial cordial.

Sasha had already decided that it couldn't possibly be for himself. Basil was such a kind soul, like his mother. He might need a potion to stand up for himself or to find some ambition, but he didn't need it to be polite.

"Just a tea party," he said. "I would invite you, of course, but it isn't my party. You understand."

"That's very kind," said Sasha.

The carriage drove past the Willow Woods, toward the part of the village that people called Upside, for being the upriver side of the two rivers that ran into each other in the village center. At the bridge over the Sweltering River, they passed the Wander Inn and the water mill.

"Should we let you out someplace?" said Basil.

"I'm good," said Sasha. "About that party—is it a fancy party?"

"Yes," said Basil.

"Are you worried about it?"

"A little."

"Do you think lots of people will come?"

"A few dozen."

Sasha peppered Basil with questions. She knew it was impolite, but she needed as much information as possible.

They passed over the bridge and went beyond the caravansary stables and the nutter's groves. If they turned left, they would have entered the village center, but they turned right, toward the Shivering River.

"Will your dad be there?" said Sasha.

"We're passing the village," said Basil.

"He seems like he doesn't like parties."

"He doesn't."

"Or people," said Sasha.

"Or animals," said Basil.

"Do you think he'll be rude to the guests?"

"Almost certainly," said Basil. "But that won't surprise anyone."

Everyone knew that Vadim Gentry was a severe man who had once fought a bear for smiling at him too much.

The carriage drove under a stone gate and arrived at the Gentry Mansion. The house was so big that it straddled the Shivering River. The black stone walls rose up into thin towers that looked like thorns.

For the first time on the trip, Sasha was struck silent.

They rode up the driveway. On either side stood columns of trees lined up like soldiers. When they pulled up to the entry, Sasha noticed maids and servants rushing around holding trays, linens, and flowers. A simple tea party at the Gentry Mansion seemed pretty complicated.

"We're here," said Basil. "I'm sorry we didn't drop you off someplace."

"That's okay," said Sasha.

As soon as they stopped, an old man in a purple tuxedo rushed out of the house and opened the carriage door. He stood straight up, as if an invisible hand was holding him by the scruff of the neck. He had white hair, a white mustache, and eyes a deep greenish brown—eyes like the Thistlewood Swamp. "You are needed inside, Master Basil," said the man. Only then did he

notice Sasha sitting in the carriage.

He looked at her as if she were a weevil in his rice. He kept looking at her but spoke to Basil. "Would you like me to set another place for your...guest?"

"Thank you, Butta," said Basil. "My friend Sasha just needed a ride into town."

Butta didn't have to say anything. His white eyebrows simply lifted, as if to say, "She missed her stop."

Sasha felt her cheeks grow hot. She had never felt so unwelcome. Maybe he was the one who needed the cordial cordial.

They stepped out of the carriage.

"You are needed urgently," said Butta.

"What is it?" said Basil.

But his answer came immediately when a window on the second floor of the house suddenly shattered and a pair of boots came flying out. Glass rained down. The boots hit the driveway not far from Sasha.

"No!" came a shout from the window. "I said I won't wear those ratty old boots, and I mean it!"

"I see," said Basil.

A face appeared in the hole where the window used to be. "Basil!"

It was Sisal Gentry, Basil's little sister. She was Sasha's age but never spoke to Sasha. "Did you see what they're trying to do to me?" She slammed the window open and climbed onto the sill. "You there," she said at a maid walking by with a tablecloth. "Yeah, you. Catch me."

Sisal jumped from the window, into the

arms of the bewildered maid. They both hit the ground, but Sisal was cushioned by the woman.

She got up and dusted herself off as she stomped toward the back garden. "Not a good catch, Martha. Come on, Basil, you have to see this."

Sisal completely ignored Sasha. And Sasha was more than happy to let her.

Everything seemed so obvious to Sasha all of a sudden. The cordial was for Sisal, the most spoiled girl in the village.

"Is the party for her?" said Sasha.

"Sort of," said Basil. "We have a tea party every harvest season. The headmistress of the Sunderdown Academy is coming. My mom wants Sisal to attend. It's a great school."

"If I were Sisal's mom, I'd send her to boarding school too."

"She's already run off a dozen tutors," said Basil. "Two of them joined the Make Mad Order—they said they'd come back to burn our house down."

Sasha made a whistling sound. "So you're hoping Sisal makes a good impression on the headmistress."

"At this point, I'm just hoping she doesn't stab the woman."

CHAPTER 4

Basil excused himself and ran after his sister. That left Sasha and Butta the butler standing beside the carriage.

Awkward silence.

"So," said Sasha, "when do the guests arrive?"

"In a few hours, which means I must unpack these groceries."

As Butta walked to the back of the carriage to unload the treats, Sasha heard rustling and grunting coming from the bags.

Uh-oh, thought Sasha. Butta approached

with caution. As soon as he opened the gate on the trunk of the carriage, the bags tumbled out, along with empty wrappers and Puck, his hair sprinkled with cookie crumbs and his lips covered in chocolate.

He smiled like a baby bear in a blueberry patch. He waved hello. Butta must have put up with a lot in the Gentry house, because though he seemed furious, he also was extremely still. Only his mustache twitched.

"Who are you?" he said to Puck.

Puck didn't say anything. Sasha ran around Butta and grabbed Puck by the hand. "He's just my—um—pet gremlin. We'll be going now."

Sasha pulled Puck and ran back down the driveway, through the columns of trees, and out the stone gate. They stopped to catch their breath. "You ate all the party supplies?" said Sasha.

Puck nodded. Then he thought about it, reached into his pocket, and pulled out a piece of honey cake squeezed into a ball and hairy with pocket fuzz.

He offered it to Sasha.

"Ew, no," said Sasha. "I mean, ew, no thank you."

That was the polite way to say it.

Which reminded Sasha of

her mission. She began to pace back and forth as Puck sat by the stone wall and ate his cake ball.

"This one seems obvious. Sisal is a spoiled brat who is rude to everyone. Her mother and brother want her to get into Sunderdown Academy. The headmistress is coming to a tea party. They're afraid she will insult the headmistress and ruin her chances. So Basil bought the cordial cordial to get Sisal into Sunderdown Academy!"

Sasha looked up from her pacing.

Puck was licking his fingers.

"Did you get all that?"

Puck nodded yes.

"Really?"

Puck shook his head no.

A few minutes later, Sasha and Puck were sneaking around the Gentry Mansion to the gardens in the back. Sisal was standing on a table shouting orders at the staff.

Sasha and Puck hid behind a rosebush.

"All we have to do is tell Sisal that the headmistress will be at the party and how great Sunderdown Academy is. Odds are she'll be dying to get in."

"Guh," said Puck.

They watched as Basil tried to help move chairs and flowerpots, so his sister wouldn't be so mean to everyone else. At one point, after screaming for an especially long time, Sisal said, "And you know what, Martha? You've been so bad today that I'm losing my voice. Is that what you wanted?"

Basil ran up to her and pulled the potion from his pocket. "Here, drink this."

"What is it?" said Sisal.

"It's a potion to make you polite to people."

"Funny," said Sisal. "And I am polite already if people would just be good at doing things and listening to me." Sisal guzzled the drink. She stuck her tongue out at Basil and made a face.

"It probably takes a while to kick in," said Basil. Basil smiled as he walked off to help the servants set more tables.

Sisal went back to giving orders.

"Okay," said Sasha, "you go to the right and make some kind of distraction. I'll go left and get Sisal's attention. I'll tell her Basil's dream for her to attend Sunderdown Academy, and we'll both get out of here as fast as possible. Ready. Go."

They ran out from behind the rosebush. Sasha ran face-first into Butta the butler. Puck ran face-first into Abrus the dog bear.

Sasha looked up.

Butta looked down.

Puck growled.

Abrus growled deeper.

There was a split second before Puck ran for his life with Abrus barking behind him, and Butta grabbed Sasha by the cuff and marched her out. In that split second, they heard Sisal shout, "I don't *care* that she's coming, Basil! Abrus gets a seat, and Princess Wisteria is the guest of honor. I want her whole saddle covered in sequins!"

"Isn't Princess Wisteria her horse?" said Sasha as Butta pushed her through the stone gate.

"Yes. Now please leave."

"She wants to throw the party for her horse?"

Butta didn't say anything.

At that moment, Puck scrambled up the stone wall and down the other side. He landed next to Sasha, panting.

"Gooby," he said, eyes wide, gulping for air. "Gooby, gooby."

Back on the other side of the wall, Abrus barked and pawed at the stones.

"Okay, time to go," said Sasha.

CHAPTER 5

Sasha and Puck walked on the dirt road, down the hill, away from the Gentry Mansion. Beside the road ran the Shivering River. It burbled over the stones and through the thrushes. Autumn had come to the village, and the air carried a chill. Otherwise, Sasha would have taken off her shoes and walked in the icy water.

Puck didn't mind the chill. He ran a zigzag across her path, from the road to the river, splashing into it like a retriever chasing a butterfly. It was as if he had already forgotten their troubles.

Sasha pulled out her detective's notebook and tried to organize her thoughts.

"Okay, our mission isn't as easy as I thought," said Sasha. "I'm willing to admit that."

"Guh!" said Puck, frolicking from river to road.

"But you have to admit you weren't much help."

"Guh."

"I know. I saw. His paws are huge."

Sasha wrote in her book:

Mission: Make Sisal polite.

Obstacles: Abrus the dog bear

She underlined "Abrus the dog bear."

Under that, she wrote: Butta the butler, who was another obstacle. Both were preventing them from getting into the Gentry Mansion.

"What else? Let's see. Even if we *could* join the party, Sisal already knows that the headmistress of that academy is coming, and she doesn't care."

Puck sent another grunt as he loped into the water.

"Right," said Sasha, "it's worse than that. She wants to throw the party for her horse, which is so rude I can't even imagine anything ruder. You know, this would be so much easier if magic were real and that cordial actually worked."

Puck didn't say anything. Sasha had the feeling that Puck, like Papa, was a hopeless believer in magic.

Magic was like a city of gold or a Cinderhoof stallion—even if they did exist, they didn't exist *here*. So it didn't matter. She had to solve the case without it.

And what was worse, this particular potion had been sold to a Gentry. Papa would never admit it, but Vadim Gentry was a villainous man. Every season, he made an offer to Papa for the deed to the shop. He didn't even want the shop, just the hill it sat on, which nestled into the Willow Woods. He would probably demolish their home and build himself a hunting lodge, so he could wander the wood looking for magical creatures to admire and then shoot. Sasha promised herself that she wouldn't fail.

As they walked beside the river, they neared the caravansary stables. A giant red-and-yellow tent swayed in the breeze beside the road. Next to it was a small paddock for horses and oxen to

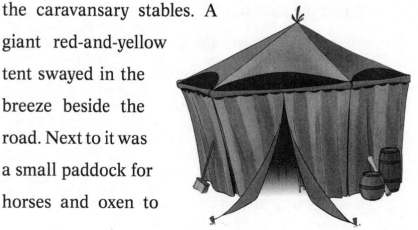

graze freely by the river and a small barn where the animals could go to hide from storms.

In the giant tent was the stabler's den. It would have a few cots to rent for a night, a table to play games like *shatranj*, and a humble offering of bottled drinks, traveler's breads, cured meats, olives, and dried fruit.

It was the kind of place a caravan would stop as they traveled through the valley, to rest their animals and sleep for a while.

It wasn't cozy, but it was dry and warm.

As soon as Puck saw the stables, he darted down the river toward them. "Wait!" said Sasha, chasing after him. Puck scurried into the tent. Sasha followed. When she entered and her eyes got used to the dark interior, she saw the stabler—a broad-shouldered woman in riding pants, with a multicolor bandana around her head holding back a ponytail as full as an actual pony's tail.

Puck was in her arms, hugging her neck. Beside them was Papa—Sasha's papa—holding a satchel full of bottles from the shop.

"Of all the odds and oddity," said Sasha, "what are you doing here?"

"I could ask the same," said Papa. He seemed almost embarrassed. "I thought you were with Basil."

"We were walking by the river," said Sasha.

"You must be Sasha," said the stabler. "Your papa was just telling me about his amazing new horse liniment."

Sasha knew the shop was having trouble. Now she realized Papa was going door-to-door to sell his oils and ointments. That was why he had been so tired in the mornings.

She walked to Papa and gave him her tightest hug. Then she said, "It's so good it's almost magic. It could probably even soothe a Cinderhoof stallion."

The stabler laughed. "Is that so?" she said, asking Puck as she held him. Puck nodded. "Then I'd be a fool if I didn't keep some around. I'll take five bottles, Master Bebbin."

Puck shook his head.

"No?" said the stabler.

He poked his thumb at the ceiling.

"More."

He nodded.

"I'll take eight bottles, then."

Puck kissed her on the cheek. She seemed like a hard woman, one who had to wrestle horses out of rivers and keep rowdy caravan drivers in line. But when Puck kissed her, she laughed and her whole barrel chest rumbled.

Papa said his thanks and put eight bottles on the table. The stabler paid in pieces of silver. In all the talk of horses and liniments, Sasha was starting to scratch at the corners of a plan. She hugged Papa one more time before he left and asked for a bottle of horse liniment.

He kissed her on the forehead as he put a bottle into her satchel. "Be careful," he said. Then he walked out, down the hill. Odds were that he was going to the stables on the other end of the village or to the farrier, who often needed to soothe horses as he put shoes on them.

After Papa left, Sasha turned to the stabler. She had put Puck down and was stacking barrels in the corner of her tent to make room for more bedrolls.

"So how do you know Puck, Miss, um, Stabler?" said Sasha.

"I know all the wanderers around these parts," said the stabler. "And the name's Oxiana. You can call me Oxi. No 'miss.'"

Sasha liked Oxi immediately. Like an ox, she was straightforward and steady. No shilly-shallying. No fuss. She stacked the last barrel and reached back toward Sasha. "Hand me that barrel tap, would ya?" She pointed at an iron cylinder lying on the table.

Sasha grabbed it and handed it to her.

Oxi patted the side of the barrel like she was checking if it was a ripe watermelon. Then she stabbed the cylinder into the side.

"Now hand me that cup, quick like," said Oxi.

Sasha sprang to attention and handed her a tin cup from the table.

Oxi held the cup beneath the tap as a stream of ruby liquid poured from the barrel. When it was full, she turned off the spigot and handed the cup to Sasha.

"Pomegranate cider from Timurlan's Orchard."

"It's delicious," said Sasha.

"People pay me with goods from all over. Here, have some dried beef with it."

She tossed Sasha a few strips of jerky. Sasha put it in her satchel for later.

"Or sometimes they pay me with news."

"Really?" said Sasha, suddenly forgetting her mission. "Do you have news of the war? I mean, are the knights winning?"

Oxi drained her cup of cider in one gulp and said, "Let me tell you something, kid. There's no winning or losing in war. There's just starting and stopping. The rest is bad news."

"Oh," said Sasha. She was rarely speechless, but all she could think about were the odds that her mother would be home again before winter.

Oxiana realized she had given a cruel answer

and said, "But wartime alchemy is mostly healing, so they probably keep your mom safe in the fortresses."

Sasha nodded and spent the rest of her energy trying not to cry. She didn't want to cry in front of Oxi, who had probably never cried.

Oxi added, "I did have a group of musicians come through who had crossed paths with cannoneers, who had just met some pearl divers from the Queen Sea. You know how the knights use pearl tips for their arrows?"

Sasha nodded. The tears were impossible to hide.

"Well, the divers told the cannoneers, who told the musicians, the Make Mad Order is retreating. Or at least the blight is receding back into their shadow gates. That has to be good, right?"

Sasha had to admit it sounded better.

"And I bet your mom is saving a lot of people."

Sasha nodded again.

"Come help me with this."

Oxi handed Sasha a terry cloth sheet to wrap on one side of a cot. "There's a caravan coming in from Rozny, and their scout says they'll pay to sleep here."

They wrapped the extra cots and put them in a row along the back of the tent.

"There," said Oxi, clapping Sasha on the back. "If you're worried about something, get some work done. Be useful. You won't have time to fret on it."

Sasha laughed. She was so thankful that Oxi hadn't mentioned her crying.

Oxi said, "And I appreciate what you've done for that boy."

"Who, Puck?" said Sasha. She realized that she'd completely forgotten about him and he wasn't anywhere in the stabler's tent.

Oxiana adjusted her head scarf with her palm and said, "Yeah, giving him food and a place to stay. Most of the villagers threw rocks at him when he arrived."

Sasha was eager to know anything about Puck. "When was that?"

"Not long ago. Maybe the war set him adrift."

"Is he...a person?"

"I don't know," said Oxi. "He seems like a fairy, the way he appears right underfoot. And he grunts like an ogre in his sleep."

"And he says 'gooby,'" added Sasha.

"Oh really?" said Oxi. "He must have learned that. But he eats like a swamp rat, and have you heard him cry? It's like a howler monkey stubbed its toe or something."

"But he's a friend to lizards," said Sasha, if only to give him one compliment. "And little creatures."

"He is, isn't he?" said Oxi, thinking about it for the first time. "Very peculiar. He slept out back for a while, in a hole in the apple tree by the river."

"Do you think he's magic?" asked Sasha.

"I think he's lonely," said Oxiana.

"Me too," said Sasha.

She said goodbye to Oxiana the stabler and walked down to the riverbank, where Puck was sitting with his feet in the water. He seemed so peaceful. Sasha wondered if he was somebody's little brother. He was eating an apple and kicking his feet to splash water. He looked as innocent as a baby bird.

It was nearly too late when she saw the rustling of a creature prowling behind a bush, ready to pounce on him.

Sasha should have screamed, but her throat seized.

She ran down the hill. But she wouldn't make it in time.

No! she thought. *No, don't hurt him!*

But before she could reach Puck or warn him, the creature leaped from the shadows onto Puck.

CHAPTER 6

"No!" shouted Sasha. "Don't—"

But by then, she saw the creature as it jumped into the daylight and landed on Puck's head. It was a mangy squirrel with a patchy tail. For half a second, Sasha thought, *Oh. It's just a squirrel. What a relief.*

Then the squirrel began to climb all over him to get at the apple.

Puck shouted, "Neh neh neh!"

The squirrel squeaked and lunged from Puck's shoulder to the apple.

"Neh neh neh!"

"Squeak squeak squeak!"

They rolled around on the riverbank, both tugging on the apple. It seemed to occur to Puck that the fight would be over if there was no apple. So he bit it.

The squirrel realized the same thing. So he chomped on.

Now they were face-to-face, biting on either side of the apple, glaring at each other. With his mouth full, Puck said, "Neh!"

The squirrel squeaked.

The insult was too great. Puck let go of the apple and tried to bite the squirrel instead. The squirrel did the same. They were both shouting and biting and scratching and rolling until Sasha ran up and said, "Stop it!"

But they didn't stop.

She would have kicked them, but they might have bitten her leg. So Sasha waited for the right moment, then pushed both of them into the icy

water of the Shivering River.

Puck yowled and ran back to shore.

The squirrel squeaked, but he was too small, and the current took him.

"Squeak!"

Puck turned and dove back into the water.

For such a dirty creature, he certainly knew how to swim. He reached the squirrel and scooped him up. He let the squirrel cling to his head as he took them both to the shore.

"I'm sorry I had to do that," said Sasha as they panted and shivered, "but you were both being unreasonable."

Puck made a complaining sound.

"Yes, you were," said Sasha.

Puck made a scoffing sound.

"Were too. It was very childish."

Puck made a questioning sound.

"*How?* Are you serious? You were killing each other for a measly apple."

Puck made a sound like she was wrong about the value of the apple. The squirrel ran onto his shoulder and added squeaks to the argument.

"You're both being silly. Don't stick your tongues out at me. Don't do it. Because. It's not about that apple. I like apples just fine. I do. But you are standing under an apple tree."

Both Puck and the squirrel stopped.

They put their tongues back in their mouths.

They looked up at the branches of the apple tree.

The branches were full of apples.

Puck and the mangy squirrel both fell back onto the grass laughing.

Sasha tried to speak, but it was no use.

They laughed and laughed.

They rolled around and patted each other until finally they got all their giggles out. Then they started to jabber at each other like they were old friends.

"Wait," said Sasha. "You two know each other?"

Puck nodded.

"Do you know more…creatures?"

Puck nodded.

"Can they help with our mission?"

"Guh," said Puck, as if that was the obvious reason he had come to the river in the first place.

He put two fingers to his mouth and blew a loud whistle. Then they waited. When Sasha looked at Puck, he bounced his eyebrows like *Just wait and see.*

Before Sasha could say anything, they heard the patter of little feet. From behind the tree trunk appeared a twitchy, one-eared chipmunk. Then a toothy rat, then a gross, old badger.

Every single one of them looked smelly and smelled sticky.

"Guh, guh!" said Puck, gesturing to the rat, chipmunk, squirrel, and badger as if he was introducing them.

"I don't speak...you," said Sasha. "Do your friends have names?"

Puck nodded, "Guh," as if he had *just* said that.

"Can I call them Toothy, Twitchy, Mangy, and Gross?"

They all shrugged.

Puck started to tell them about Abrus. As he spoke, his eyes grew large. He pointed at his teeth and pretended to swipe at them with his claws. He made fierce gestures, as if describing a ferocious battle with a gigantic beast.

The gang of fur nodded and offered suggestions.

When they were all settled with their plan, they huddled together and touched their foreheads to one another in a circle.

When they broke the huddle, the four creatures took off in different directions and disappeared.

Puck smiled at Sasha and gave her a thumbs-up.

"I have no idea what you just did, but does this mean they'll help us with Abrus?"

Puck nodded, and they started to walk back to the stables.

Sasha felt the need to fill the silence. "Good. Okay. Good job. Sorry about pushing you in the river. I thought the mangy squirrel was a stranger. Did you really used to sleep here? Can they really be trusted?"

Puck didn't say anything, but Sasha knew he could be trusted, so she didn't press the issue. Besides, they had Butta the Butler to worry about.

And the party would be starting soon. They needed a plan to get past him and another plan to make Sisal act right.

As they crested the hill, she saw a caravan of horses and pack mules pulling into the stables—the caravan from Rozny.

The headmistress would be with them. And from the other road, they saw Basil's carriage there to pick up the headmistress, to take her to the party.

"Uh-oh," said Puck.

"Uh-oh," said Sasha.

They were out of time.

CHAPTER 7

As they ran back up the hill, Sasha worked on her plan. She would need the help of Basil and Oxiana. And that gang of fur would have to be able to take orders. And even then, the headmistress would have to be carefully monitored. And who knew what Sisal would do? She was completely out of control. But if everything else went right, then maybe the plan would work.

The odds weren't good.

But it was all she had.

Sasha turned to Puck and said, "Quick, run to Oxiana and make sure she doesn't go anywhere before we can ask a favor."

Puck put his palm up to one eye, a knight's salute, and then ran toward the stabler's tent. Already, it looked overrun with men and women from the caravan leading their animals into the stables, unloading their saddle packs, and barking commands at one another. Puck skittered between their legs and disappeared into the tent.

Sasha veered toward the Gentry carriage, where Basil was standing in his formal attire, holding a bottle of iced hibiscus tea.

"Hi, Basil!"

Basil laughed uncomfortably.

"I bet you're wondering what I'm doing here," said Sasha.

"That'd be impolite to ask," said Basil.

"But I bet you were thinking it."

Basil laughed again.

"Is that tea for the headmistress?"

"It is."

"Are you taking her in the carriage?"

"I am."

"You have such nice horses," said Sasha. She patted each horse on the neck. As she did, she secretly drew the bottle of horse liniment from her satchel and rubbed a tiny amount on each one. The horses seemed to like the cold sensation. They nuzzled Sasha's hand for more.

Soon, they would start to feel relaxed. And by the time Basil and the headmistress got into the carriage, the horses would be almost asleep. That would buy Sasha some time to work on the rest of her plan. But first, she had to get into the mansion.

First, she stalled a little more by asking a dozen questions about the headmistress and her

school. Then, after Basil began to get bored, she said, "I was wondering, do you think I could attend the party?" Sasha tried to offer her very best, most charming smile. "I could even help clean up if you want."

Basil had been polite in every way. Surely he would not be so rude now to refuse a guest. "I'm sorry," said Basil, squirming in discomfort and wrung his hands. "I can't. The invitations are set."

Sasha was embarrassed that she'd asked.

"It's okay," she said.

"But if someone was to find my ring and return it, then the only right thing to do would be to let her join the party."

Sasha was confused for a moment.

"Your ring?" she said.

"Yes, that's right."

He was playing with a silver ring engraved with the Gentry seal.

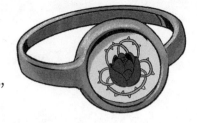

"That ring?" said Sasha.

"Yep," said Basil. "I lost it."

He winked.

Then he made a show of dropping it in the dirt and walking away toward the stabler's tent. "You must be Headmistress Salima," said Basil to a woman wearing a big red hat, walking toward them.

Sasha quickly pocketed the ring and ran past, hoping the headmistress wouldn't look too closely. If her plan worked, she would meet the headmistress later on. For now, she had solved the problem of Butta the butler.

"Thank you, Basil," shouted Sasha as she ducked into Oxiana's tent. "You're a gentle friend!"

Sasha rushed past the caravaneers. Many of them were sitting in circles, playing music on lutes and singing songs that Sasha didn't recognize. Over the hubbub, she heard Oxiana's gruff voice.

"And will *somebody* find that Bebbin girl!"

Sasha squeezed through the crowd, wondering what she could have possibly done to make Oxi sound so mad at her. Then she got her answer. Oxiana the stabler was overrun with customers who wanted to rent cots and buy pomegranate cider, but she was stuck in place. Puck had wrapped himself around her ankles and was holding on with all his might. Sasha remembered that she had asked him to make sure Oxi didn't go anywhere. Puck had taken the request seriously.

"You!" said Oxiana when she saw Sasha. "Get him off me!"

CHAPTER 8

"Down, Puck!" said Sasha, but he clung tight to Oxi's legs.

"Release!"

"I command you, release!"

"Mission complete."

Finally, Sasha knelt down beside him. His eyes were shut tight. He was trembling. Maybe all the shouting in the tent and the attention had scared him. Sasha touched him on the shoulder, but he winced. "It's okay," she whispered. "I'm not mad. Nobody's mad."

Puck opened his eyes. They were so big and curious. And they wanted so badly to please. Sasha was struck suddenly by the thought that she had been scolding him all day. She didn't mean to. He just never listened. And made such messes. And—

Sasha caught herself. She had to admit she was wrong. It was unjust to scold Puck all the time. He was only ever trying to help her.

Sasha leaned close, so their foreheads were touching. She looked him in the eyes and said, "You're doing a great job, Puck. I think you're a really great partner."

Puck's questioning look gave way to a smile full of every joy a bird can sing. He let go of Oxi's ankles and hugged Sasha's face, rubbing his nose against hers.

It took all of Sasha's strength not to scream

and wipe her face.

She could feel the dirt smearing on her nose and forehead. Was he *made* of dirt? Puck let go eventually, and she stood up.

Oxiana was up there, still angry, still wondering why in the world Puck had attached himself to her.

"Oh. Right," said Sasha. "Is now a good time to ask a favor?"

"Does this *look* like a good time?" said Oxi. She gestured at the tent hall—people everywhere, complaining in a dozen languages, dogs, monkeys, parrots, all squawking in their own.

Sasha gathered herself. "Right. It's never a good time to ask a favor, which is why now is as good a time as any."

Oxiana had to laugh at the absurd logic.

She set out twelve tin cups and said, "Fill these with cider while you talk. Then I'll listen."

Sasha grabbed the first cup and put it under the spigot.

"Okay. We don't have much time. I only need you for a few minutes."

"That sounds easy enough," said Oxi.

"But those minutes are now."

"Okay, what do you need?"

"And they're not here."

"Where are they?"

"At the Gentry Mansion."

"Not a chance," said Oxi. She handed a few of the full cups to a merchant in exchange for a coin.

"It'll be super quick."

"No."

"You don't have to do much."

"Sorry, kid."

"I'll do all the talking."

"I believe you."

"So you'll do it?"

"No."

"Okay, what if Puck and I come back and help you with the caravans? He can watch the horses, and I'm a very good shopkeeper."

That was an offer that got Oxi's attention. The caravan was bigger than usual, and she'd need all the help she could get.

Sasha knew when she had made a sale. She stayed quiet while Oxiana thought it over. The only worry was if Oxi could leave her stables unattended. Sasha added, "We'll even shovel out the stable."

Oxiana was practically a giant. So when she stepped onto a table, everyone stopped and looked, wondering how long the table legs would hold out. Oxi cleared her throat and said, "Listen up. I'm leaving for a few minutes. I counted my coins and I counted the cups left in the cider barrels. If you want one, take it and leave a coin. Otherwise, don't touch anything."

Everyone gaped up at her, mouths open.

"Got it?" she said.

Everyone nodded.

She got off the table. It creaked with relief.

Then Oxi walked to her cabinet and pulled out a coat made of a lion skin. She swung it over her shoulders, so the lion's mouth rested on her head like a hood.

"Okay," she

said. "Let's ride."

She started toward the tent entrance.

"Wait," said Sasha. "Do you have a different coat by any chance?"

She looked at the fearsome lion skin on Oxiana's shoulders. "This favor is a bit more... um...delicate."

"I have one made out of a crocodile face," said Oxi.

"How about we forget coats altogether?"

Oxi shrugged the coat off her shoulders.

"It's your show, little lady."

CHAPTER 9

They rode Oxiana's fastest horse up the hill toward the Gentry Mansion. It was a beige charger, fit to ride into battle, so tall that Sasha felt a little dizzy. She sat with Puck in the front, and Oxiana sat behind them to make sure they didn't fall off. But the horse was so thick that Sasha and Puck could have sat side by side. They could have had their own tea party on the broad horse.

On the road, they passed the Gentry carriage. It was stopped on the side. Three of the horses were fast asleep. The windows of carriage were shuttered. The driver had his hands on his head, wondering what to do.

It worked! The horse liniment worked! thought Sasha.

But the horses would wake up eventually, so they had to hurry.

"When we get there," said Sasha, "I might say some things that seem strange."

"No kidding," said Oxi.

"Just go with it, okay?" They galloped under the stone gate.

Oxiana said, "I've got ten minutes before the caravaneers start stealing everything that isn't nailed down in my stables. And fifteen minutes before they start on the nails. Till then, I'm all yours."

"Okay," said Sasha. "But just try to be, I dunno, classy sounding."

The horse pulled up in front of the mansion with a whiny and snort. Oxiana jumped off and helped Sasha down. Puck got down by swinging off the bridle.

Oxi said, "Classy sounding, got it."

"Like you're a princess who was a middle child and so you started an academy in the mountains for rich girls to learn astronomy and falconry and secret arts. But you're still kinda stuffy."

"That's really specific," said Oxiana.

"And your name's Salima. Follow me."

They walked around the house to the gardens in the back, where they could hear the hubbub of the party.

They were back at the rosebush they had hidden behind that morning, but this time, they had a ring and a gang of fur and a broad-shouldered stabler.

Sasha took a deep breath. Then she knelt down and looked at Puck. "Are you ready?"

"Guh!" said Puck.

"Good luck," said Sasha. She whispered the plan into his ear, to make sure he remembered.

Puck nodded. Then he put both hands to his mouth like a trumpet and made a birdcall. "Kulu koo koo!"

Sasha watched as the gang of fur—Toothy, Twitchy, Mangy, and Gross—climbed over the stone wall like invading barbarians.

Puck made a few hand signals, and the creatures disappeared into the bushes surrounding the garden party.

As Puck ran around the bush to find the dog bear Abrus, Sasha thought she could hear him giggling.

It took only a few seconds to find out why. Puck had made it as far as the first table of the outdoor banquet. Abrus, who was seated at the main table next to Sisal, spotted him immediately.

The dog bear barked and sprang into action. Puck grabbed the tablecloth and bolted away, sending a dozen trays of tea cookies into the air.

Sasha and Oxi stayed hidden behind the rosebush. Puck sprinted past them, dragging the cloth behind him. Abrus was not too far behind that.

But as soon as Abrus crossed the hedge of roses, the trap was set. The gang of fur jumped out of the bushes and onto Abrus. They were measly things next to the great big dog, but they looked like the kind of creatures who had been in a few scrapes.

Toothy the rat nipped at the dog's ears, Mangy the squirrel covered his eyes, Gross the badger held his back leg, and Twitchy the chipmunk jumped on his snout, held fast, and head-butted Abrus over and over, in a wild puff of rage.

It was all enough distraction for Puck to throw the tablecloth over Abrus. Together, the five smaller creatures managed to bundle the dog bear with enough cloth left over to wrap around his snout so he couldn't make any noise. Then they dragged him into a shady corner of the garden wall.

"Wow," said Oxiana. "That was aggressive and adorable at the same time."

"Our turn," said Sasha. She took Oxi by the hand and walked toward the party.

It was the most lavish party that Sasha had ever seen. The green lawn was surrounded by black tulips in flower beds. Tables with white tablecloths held a feast of orange blossom honey cakes, sesame brittle, and candied rose petals. Three copper samovars stood on a bed of hot coals in the center of a stone firepit. Each was brewing a different kind of tea. The teacups were delicate porcelain, painted with lacy flower patterns. Guests wandered from table to table chatting. A troupe of bards from Rozny played a quartet of harps and sang the "Ballad of Knights and Days."

If Sasha wasn't so busy, she would have been mesmerized by all the beautiful things. But her vision was quickly blocked by the figure of Butta the butler.

CHAPTER 10

"We've done this before," said Butta with a sigh. "You must leave now."

Oxiana the stabler had dealt with much tougher customers in her work. She said, "I think you mean to say we must leave now, *please*. To be polite and all."

Butta rolled his eyes but did what she said. "Very well. You must leave now, please."

"No," said Oxiana.

"What?" said Butta.

"I guess you're right," said Oxiana. "I should

have said no, *thank you.*"

Butta's neck became red and his lips clenched.

Before he could shout for more guards, Sasha stepped forward. "Hi, Mr. Butta. We're sorry to bother, but we're not here for the party. We're here to speak with Basil."

"He's not here."

"That's okay. We'll wait by the cake table."

"I'm sorry," said Butta. But before he could finish, Sasha pulled Basil's seal ring from her pocket.

"Basil said to show you this," said Sasha.

Butta's eyes became as wide as teacups. But there was nothing more to say. The Gentry seal was the final authority for the butler.

He stepped aside.

"Come on," said Sasha. They had very little time. Sasha and Oxiana rushed into the crowded party. Vadim Gentry was surrounded by the mayor, the constable, and a few other bigwigs. They snuck past and found Sisal at her table. She was commanding a maid to braid her horse's tail. The maid was trying to obey without getting kicked. To Sasha's surprise, Princess Wisteria was a squat and dumpy horse with shaggy hair. Sasha would have expected Sisal to have a fancy show pony. But she supposed that Vadim Gentry knew his own daughter would only treat the creature like a dress-up doll. And even though Sisal

was his favorite child, he wasn't about to waste money on that. After all, money was Vadim Gentry's favorite anything in the whole world.

As soon as Sisal saw them, she put down her cake, stood up, and pounded on the table.

"Who said you could be here?"

"I just came to say happy birthday," said Sasha.

"It's not my birthday, dum-dum. Why would I have all these adults at my birthday party?"

"Sorry, I just figured the party was for you."

"Of course it's for me—me and Princess Wisteria. And Abrus, but he ran off 'cause he's trained to protect me. That braid looks super sloppy, Martha."

Oxiana leaned over to Sasha and said, "Is this little child for real?"

Sasha whispered, "Stay classy, remember?" Then she raised her voice to say, "Well, Miss Salima, it was nice to meet you, but I guess I was wrong about the birthday. Silly me."

"Did you say Salima?" said Sisal.

"Yeah, why?" said Sasha.

Sisal ignored Sasha and spoke to Oxi. "Are you the headmistress of Sunderdown Academy?"

"Uh," said Oxi, looking to Sasha for help. "Who wants to know?"

It wasn't the classy kind of answer a headmistress would give, but Sisal went on.

"*I'm* the reason my brother brought you here. So you could invite me to your little school. But you should know I don't go anywhere without Princess Wisteria. And I get my own room. And, you know what, this is going to be a long list. I'll have Butta send you some paperwork."

"I'll give you paperwork," grumbled Oxi under her breath.

"You don't *look* like a princess," said Sisal.

"What do I look like?" said Oxi.

"I don't know. What kind of people make bathtubs? You look like that."

Sasha stepped in front of Oxiana before she could flip Sisal's entire table over. "All right," said Sasha, "I'm sure Salima has things to discuss with your parents."

"You bet I do," said Oxi.

Sasha made a gesture, and Oxi stomped off. Oxiana had done her part of the plan perfectly, and now she could head back to her stable. She marched across the garden without even a nod to the other guests. Vadim stood unsmiling in the center, like a dark tower. He watched Oxiana leave, then traced her path back to Sasha. For a moment, he stared at Sasha, as if to ask, *What are you doing here?* Sasha turned away and hoped he would too.

Sisal had already moved on to order Martha around, but Sasha had one last part to her plan. This was the big moment, and it had to go just right.

"Hey, Sisal," said Sasha, "I was just coming up the hill, and I think your brother was escorting a surprise guest."

"I know," said Sisal with a sneer. "It was the headmistress who just left. But I don't care about her school, so whatever."

"But it didn't look like her," said Sasha. "This guest was wearing a big red hat. Do you think she could be Edmi Strasspluss?" Sasha said the name with a tone of wonder and amazement. She sounded out the name slowly—*Ed-mee Strass-plus*—as if it belonged to some legendary figure.

"Who's Edmi Strasspluss?" said Sisal.

"I heard she's the greatest horse trainer in the whole world. She was born on horseback in the hill country and can speak the whinnying language of the Cinderhooves and the Bloomhooves."

"No way," said Sisal. "Really?"

"That's what I heard."

Sasha watched as Toothy the rat climbed up the tablecloth, near where Sisal was sitting. He was right on time. The rat looked like a pirate climbing a ship's mast. But instead of a knife between his teeth, he had a little stone from one of the flower beds. Sasha tried to keep Sisal distracted. "Do you think Basil would invite a world-famous horse trainer?"

"For sure," said Sisal, popping a tea cookie into her mouth. "He totally loves me the most."

Toothy had boarded the table and was crouched right under Sisal's elbow. Only Princess Wisteria saw him, and her snort went unnoticed. Toothy waited for Sisal to lift her hand, then quickly spit the stone onto one of the cookies left on the plate. He patted it down, so

it was embedded into the cookie, like an almond. Then he dove off the table undetected. Sasha was almost certain the rat winked at her before he jumped. But she still had her part to do.

"Wow," she said. "I bet if you are nice to her, she'll teach you how to whisper a Cinderhoof incantation into Princess Wisteria's ear."

"What'll that do?" said Sisal.

"I don't know," said Sasha.

"Also, why are you even here again?"

Sasha didn't have a good answer. But she didn't need one. Sisal tossed another cookie into her mouth and bit down.

"Ow!" Sisal held her cheek and spit out the stone. "Did you thee that?" she said. "I hit a rock and bit mah tongue."

Sisal screamed and called for Martha to come inspect all the cookies.

That left Princess Wisteria unattended. Sasha made a quick whistling sound to signal Puck. A second later, Puck emerged from under a table holding the bottle of horse liniment in his mouth. He had probably learned that from Toothy. But as Puck climbed onto Princess Wisteria to apply the liniment, he must have bitten down too hard, because the bottle cap popped off and poured liniment all over him.

"Crumbsy bumsy!" said Sasha under her breath. Puck's eyes grew wide. He had just spilled horse tranquilizer all over himself. He looked around in a panic. Then he did the only thing he could do. He jumped on Princess Wisteria and rubbed his face all over.

The fancy horse snorted. She had never been hugged by a creature like Puck. Puck did his

best to transfer as much of the liniment onto Princess Wisteria as he could. Then his head nodded to the side, his eyes closed, and he fell off the horse into a flower bed.

Sasha ran over to check on him.

Puck was already asleep.

He would probably start snoring soon.

Sasha knew she needed to hurry.

When she turned to run back, she saw Basil and the headmistress heading toward Sisal.

The headmistress was a tall, thin, and pointy-faced woman. Sasha could tell she was once a princess because her clothes looked very expensive. And because she had a mustache of fine hairs and no one must have had the courage to tell her.

Thankfully, she was still wearing her red hat.

Sasha bolted toward them and stopped just in front of Basil. "Hi, Basil, what kept you?"

Basil seemed a little embarrassed. "Uh, we had some horse trouble."

Ooh, that's good. I'll have to use that later,

thought Sasha. "We've had a great time here. Your sister is a wonderful host."

"She is?" said Basil.

"Yep. Would you mind introducing me to your guest?"

"Sure. Headmistress Salima, this is my friend Sasha Bebbin."

Sasha made a bow to the headmistress and stuck her hand out for a firm handshake. "Very nice to meet you, Headmistress."

The older woman smiled. "What a proper young lady," she said.

"I learned everything from my friend Sisal. May I take you to meet her?"

"If you don't mind," said the headmistress.

"It would be an honor," said Sasha. "Just one moment."

Sasha sidled up to Basil and gestured so he would bend down and she could whisper.

"Listen, Basil. Thank you for the ring." She handed him the ring. "I didn't want to say this in front of the headmistress, but I think there's an emergency with Abrus."

"Really?"

Sasha nodded. "I saw him wrestling around in a tablecloth over by the wall. He could probably use your help."

She reached into her satchel and pulled out the strip of dried beef that Oxiana had given her. "And would you give him this when you see him? Tell him it's from me. He'll know what it's for."

"Okay," said Basil. He was too worried for the dog bear to ask about the apology beef. "I'm sorry to ask you this, but would you mind watching over Sisal and the headmistress? I really hope it goes well. I mean, the cordial cordial should be kicking in any minute now."

"Oh definitely," said Sasha, patting him on the back. "It's an extremely, um, effective potion. And I'll handle the rest."

Basil made his apologies to the headmistress and ran off to find Abrus. That left Sasha and the headmistress. At the other end of the garden, Sisal was just finished shouting at Martha to go get her ice for her mouth. Sasha made sure the headmistress didn't see. She waited for Martha to run past. She then turned and offered her hand to the headmistress. "Shall we?"

As they walked, Sasha confided in the headmistress. "Sisal is a wonderful candidate for your school. She's very excited to meet you."

"I'll be the judge," said the headmistress.

"The only thing is that she's very nervous. And when she gets nervous, she sometimes calls herself Princess Wisteria."

"But she's not a princess," said the head-mistress.

"Not like you, but you can imagine that some girls wish they could be."

"Naturally."

"It's just a nervous habit. I'm sure she'll become much more confident at the academy."

"Hmm," said the headmistress.

That was the best Sasha could do. She had set everything up for one polite conversation. She cringed to think of all that could go wrong. But she had come this far. She glanced at Princess Wisteria, who was starting to nod off a little. The liniment had made her drowsy at least. The horse didn't notice the gang of fur sneaking up, each holding a metal poker in their teeth. The metal pokers were from the firepits beneath the samovars of tea. They were used to stir the hot coals underneath, and their tips glowed orange with intense heat.

The gang of fur had stolen four of the fire brands and approached the horse, ready to execute the plan.

"Here goes nothing," said Sasha with a nervous sigh.

CHAPTER 11

Sasha and the headmistress of Sunderdown Academy approach Sisal, who was holding her cheek since she had bitten her tongue. Sasha presented Sisal and said, "Headmistress, please let me introduce Sisal Gentry. Sisal, this is the great woman we talked about before."

Sisal was a bit more subdued, since her mouth hurt, but she was still curious.

"Are you the famous Edmi Straspluss? Tell me."

"What did she say?" said the headmistress.

Sasha whispered, "Are you the famous headmistress, please tell me. She just speaks a little funny."

The headmistress made a curious look but chose not to think on it too much. "I am," she said.

"Good," said Sisal. "Then, Edmi Straspluss, can you teach Princess Wisteria to have Cinderhooves?"

It was practically a demand from Sisal. But thankfully, the headmistress heard only a request, with a please and everything. When Sisal said, "Edmi Straspluss," it sounded kind of like she was mumbling "headmistress please." And that made a whole lot more sense that the silly name, so everyone heard what they wanted to hear.

"I can," said the headmistress. "All the girls I teach will have fire beneath their feet—the fire of determination."

Sisal seemed pleased with that answer.

The headmistress seemed pleased that Sisal was so intent to learn.

But now, Sisal expected the headmistress to instruct the horse. Sasha had to think fast. She said, "You came from a place with lots of horses, didn't you?"

She knew that Sisal would think she meant the Hill Country, where Cinderhooves roamed. And the headmistress would simply assume she

was talking about the caravan she had taken down the mountain from her school. "I did," said the headmistress.

"Did you speak with anyone on your travels?"

"They don't speak," said the headmistress, referring to the caravaneers, who only spoke faraway languages.

But Sisal imagined she was talking about the horses. She said, "Princess Wisteria would love to speak with you. She's very clever if you just give her a chance."

The headmistress gave Sisal a kind look. She was thinking Sisal must have been terribly nervous. Sasha stepped in once again, "And the ride up. Basil said you had some trouble."

"Yes. The horses seem very sleepy here."

"Not mine," said Sisal. But they all looked and saw Princess Wisteria, asleep on her feet.

The headmistress made a clicking noise with her tongue, a sound of disapproval. And that was all Twitchy the chipmunk needed as his cue. Each of the gang of fur was holding on to the far side of the horse's legs. At the sound of the clicking, Twitchy bit Princess Wisteria with all his might.

The horse jolted awake, as if the headmistress had commanded it, and whinnied back at her.

"Wow!" said Sisal.

Princess Wisteria took off at a trot, and as she ran, the ground where she had stepped was scorched. It seemed impossible to believe that such a lumpy, old horse would ever run as fast as a Cinderhoof, but to Sisal, it was real. The Cinderhoof incantation had worked.

To Sasha, it was the gang of fur holding on to each leg, burning the grass with the fiery pokers that had been lying in the hot coals.

"Edmi Straspluss, I want to know *everything*," said Sisal. Sisal gave a slight bow of respect to the woman. A Cinderhoof trainer was just about the only person Sisal admired in the world.

The headmistress smiled as Sisal ran to catch up with her newly magic horse.

That was all Sasha needed to hear. She pulled the headmistress away and said over her shoulder, "Well, we must be going now. We don't want to miss our ride. Horses around these parts are always falling asleep."

The headmistress nodded. She didn't want to miss the caravan back up the mountains. "Thank you so much for coming," said Sasha as she escorted the headmistress across the garden.

"You're both very curious little girls," said the headmistress.

"Better than incurious little girls," said Sasha.

"Agreed."

The headmistress stopped. She looked into Sasha's eyes. "Young lady, I know what you did just now."

"You do?" said Sasha. She wondered if her whole plan was for nothing, if she'd failed completely.

"I do," said the headmistress. "You helped your nervous friend in her interview, even though you were both terrified. It was obvious."

"It was?"

"It was. It was also obvious that you're very kind."

The headmistress looked at Sasha with the warm approval that princesses and queens only offer on rare occasions. "You are both welcome to the Sunderdown Academy. That is, if you can manage to find a reliable horse to bring you."

Sasha laughed. "Thank you," she said.

With that, the headmistress walked toward the Gentry carriage to take her home. Sasha waited until the headmistress turned the corner. Then she sprinted back to the flower bed to check on Puck.

CHAPTER 12

Sasha scooped Puck into her arms. He was still sound asleep.

Sasha shook him a little. "You slept through all of it, gooby."

"You gooby!" said Puck. Then he nuzzled into her and went back to sleep. It had been a long day. Sasha looked around, but the gang of fur had disappeared over the garden wall. Princess Wisteria was still confused but unharmed, chewing on a few tulips.

Martha had brought the ice for Sisal's cheek.

The party was merry and hadn't noticed anything. Sasha carried Puck toward the gate.

"Wait!"

Sasha turned.

It was Basil. "I just wanted to say thank you. Sisal was really polite because of you."

Sasha hesitated.

"Because of your potion, I mean."

"Right. Yes. It must have been the sassafras. And did you find Abrus?"

"I did. Thanks for the beef."

"Anytime," said Sasha.

"Can I give you a ride home? We have several carriages," said Basil.

"No thank you," said Sasha.

She had had enough of horses and garden parties and carriages for a while.

CHAPTER 13

Sasha walked past the stabler's tent. The sun was setting, and the caravan had overrun the place. Through the open entryway, she could see Oxiana walking between the tables, placing cups of pomegranate cider. The musicians played merry songs about elvish queens who rode Bloomhooves to midnight dances in the meadow in the heart of a foggy wood.

She walked across the bridge, past the miller's house, and up the hill toward home. Maybe it was the sunset glow, but the trees of the Willow Woods looked fully orange and red.

When she arrived at the Juicy Gizzard, Sasha walked around the back, so she could make sure the chickens were safe in their coop and Otto was asleep in his pigpen. She laid Puck in his bed by the back door. He made a chirping noise and tried to hold on to her neck. She peeled him off and hummed a comforting sound that she remembered her mother making.

As Sasha entered, she saw Papa in his reading chair. Mama's reading chair was beside it, empty for now.

Papa set his glasses on his book and said, "Did you manage it?"

"Manage what?" said Sasha.

"To make that young lady polite for once in her life."

How did he know? thought Sasha. It made her feel protected to know that he had been watching over her. She said, "I think so."

"That's good," said Papa.

"Are you mad?" she said.

"Sweet bird, why would I be mad?"

"Because I didn't believe your cordial cordial would work."

Papa shrugged and smiled. "I'm not mad at all. As far as I'm concerned, the cordial worked perfectly." He winked.

Sasha thought about it for a moment. She supposed that it was possible. Maybe the only reason Sisal hadn't kicked her out was because the cordial softened her mood a little. It didn't sound plausible. But she couldn't prove it. Sasha laughed. They would each believe what they believed.

Sasha ran over and gave Papa a good-night hug.

"At least your liniment worked," she said. "Puck's still snoring out back."

Papa nodded and hugged her back. "See? We'll be rich in no time."

"I got a job at the stables. Maybe Oxi will let me keep the tips?"

Papa held Sasha's cheeks. She rarely saw his eyes this close without his glasses. They had a sparkle but deep, deep in a dark pool of night water. He looked directly into hers and smiled.

"I'm proud of you," he said.

Sasha nodded.

"Me too," she said. "I am too."

She meant she was proud of him too, but it came out muddled. She yawned. She was exhausted. She climbed into Papa's chair with him and curled up under his arm to fall asleep.

The next morning, she and Puck would help out in the stables. But first, she would tell Puck thank you for his help. It was the polite thing to do. They were friends after all.

100 Years of

Albert Whitman & Company

1919–2019

Albert Whitman & Company encompasses all ages and reading levels, including board books, picture books, early readers, chapter books, middle grade, and YA

Present

2017

The Boxcar Children celebrates its 75th anniversary and the second Boxcar Children movie, *Surprise Island*, is scheduled to be released

The first Boxcar Children movie is released

2014

2008

John Quattrocchi and employee Pat McPartland buy Albert Whitman & Company, continuing the tradition of keeping it independently owned and operated

Losing Uncle Tim, a book about the AIDS crisis, wins the first-ever Lambda Literary Award in the Children's/YA category

1989

1970

The first Albert Whitman issues book, *How Do I Feel?* by Norma Simon, is published

Three states boycott the company after it publishes *Fun for Chris*, a book about integration

1956

1942

The Boxcar Children is published

Pecos Bill: The Greatest Cowboy of All Time wins a Newbery Honor Award

1938

1919

Albert Whitman & Company is started

Albert Whitman begins his career in publishing

Early 1900s

Celebrate with us in 2019!
Find out more at www.albertwhitman.com.